I LOVE my brother ENKI

I LOVE my brother
ENKI

Astral Conversations with myself.

KN LN

First Printing Beltane 2019
ISBN: 978-1-9990839-08

This book is dedicated to Tesla.

I owe this young woman more than my life.

Without her I would not have had the space to write this story about dropping hate, finding the Balance, and opening the 3rd Gate.

Contents

KN LN

I LOVE my brother ENKI

5

Prologue

Is this the beginning?

 K. This is not the start. This is somewhere in the middle. The book I have been writing is now being tossed.

I LOVE my brother ENKI

I will be writing down my lessons here, unloading as much as I can, for as long as I can.

My thoughts are now scattered. There will be no rhyme or reason to these musings. I will jump all over. I will not attempt to follow any known style. Sometimes it may seem that I am going nowhere, it will all be relevant in the end.

I hope this inspires you to follow your dreams in this life. Enlighten the chunk of conscious energy you claim as your soul.

This is not truth. This is not fiction. This is written to get you to start thinking, so you can stop thinking. This is written for your soul.

KN LN

I LOVE my brother ENKI

Chapter 1

My first memories

The first memory I have had come to me in a dream. Maybe that is not the correct beginning?

I LOVE my brother ENKI

Let me start with dreams. I hardly ever had dreams until I was 30. If I did dream, it was vivid, alive, and it was 100% real. This would only occur a few times a year. I would remember these dreams forever. They were of the past. They were of the future. They were always true. They were impossible to change. I relived these moments.

I awoke from a dream. I was dreaming of being in a crib. My human parents were leaning over me. My mom had curly hair.

This is the youngest memory I have from this lifespan. I have unlocked memories from the consciousness grid that go all the way back to Sumer, what a place! This is not about those memories; this is about the start of this lifetime. The only lifetime that really matters.

After this dream, I contacted my mother. She is an empath and has had spirits following her around for years. I told her about the dream. She confirmed the house and time, as she had only had her hair like that once, and I had never seen it like that.

I am not sure when this dream came to me. It was in the first major cycle of this life, the first 12 years.

Things like this came to me often. I will not bore you with any of the details, as it is not relevant to these writings. The important part to take from these words was that I was in training. I was being trained to dream, and to take my dreams seriously. The dream world is akin to the astral plane. Your mind is asleep when you access this, there is no control. In later years I learned that I was being guided by my guardian through these experiences. He left me more than 5 years ago, but that story is for another day.

As I grew older, I did not understand the others. I did not keep friends. I played with all humans as if they were toys. I wanted drama. I wanted to gauge others by their actions, so I acted in many unfavorable ways. I learnt quickly to copy emotions. I could see through all lies. I never called anyone on them. I would rather let it progress to further evaluate the others in this life. I would roll with a lie to endless extremes, just for the discovery, just to see the experiment through to the end.

This way of life got me into some serious problems. I had bad anxiety around large groups of people. I could only function with others one on one. I could not shut up in a group. I only understood that talking promoted talking. I would share non-stop, thinking it would inspire others to share as well. Social skills...

The 'friends' I would hang with would in turn join the mob when it came time to pick on me. This was anything from being spat on, kicked, tied up outside in the woods overnight, force fed wild mushrooms, whipped with bicycle tires, thrown out of tree forts. It was my closest toys that I allowed to do this. I hardly fought back, but it took me years to hide the temper that followed after letting these human experiments run their course. I am trapped in this human body and I do suffer from the same chemical emotions you do. I came here in

I LOVE my brother ENKI

exile to experience them with no memory of my past. I came
here to evaluate. I came here to get ready for my next role. I
considered no one my friend. I never hated any of these
people. Not truly. I have said I did. I have acted in ways to
appear as if I was upset. I cried. I propagated these emotions
alone for days even. I did what would be expected.

Somehow, I ended up in high school. I was taken under the
wing of a few folk who stopped these violent experiments from
happening to me. A new experiment began.

I was smart in school. I never did any homework. I did not
pay attention in class. I was stoned around the clock so I could
meditate in class and do my real learning. I did not take notes.
I would figure out how to do the quiz during the quiz. I was an
'A' student. I did not fit in any of the groups. I did not add any
real friends to my life. I had experiments running in every part
of my town, in every group of friends, in every aspect of life.

I grew up out of town, surrounded by farms. I was an
outdoorsy kid smoking cigarettes in the forest at 10, blowing up
shit, and shooting ground squirrels for the farmers. In the
early years of my life I discovered the mountains. Skiing was a
winter favorite from 3 years old. Snowboarding came into my
life soon after. Getting high, drugs and summits, turns and
jumps, this was how to feel elevated. This was how to feel
correct. Activity. I found meditation in a way no ever described
to me.

I had been doing yoga and meditating from elementary
school on my own. It never clicked. I knew I was supposed to

be doing it daily. My ADHD was far too out of control to be successful at it. I found it in activity. The more I could zone out, the easier it was to leave my body and learn. Meditation is learning. Books are actually worthless. If you meditate, you can converse with the source and cover far more ground. Time is all we have while here. Time is relative, and in the astral plane I can move at the speed of light and slow it down. I can squeeze days of conversations in less than an hour with my eyes closed. I usually do not get to choose the lessons. Those are chosen for me.

The original idea for this book was these stories from my youth. They lay a great foundation for the rest of my life and I will be revisiting them as this story unfolds. The main focus will be what I have learnt. The focus is to get you to think, and then to realize that those thoughts are not you.

To inspire you to enlighten that chunk of conscious energy you call your soul, is my goal. Drop the materials. Drop the lust for wealth and power. Power corrupts the unbalanced soul. ENKI is about to take power again. ENLIL's time as the leader of the 6 for the 7th is nigh. The world will begin anew soon, as it is foretold. You can take these writings seriously, but I would not recommend it. This is just the fictitious and entertaining version. Do not take these musings to heart. Meditate and ask ENKI what is up, he may just talk to you.

I LOVE my brother ENKI

Chapter 2

Tarot

 mentioned before that this may be all the fuck over the place. My brain is completely scattered. Time is... too much.

I LOVE my brother ENKI

I was told to get to my experience with tarot card readings
out of the way. I suppose it will set the groundwork for some
much needed background. There were no lessons last night, so
I figure that this needs to be out before my own learning can
continue.

I actually grew up under a Lutheran mother. My father is
Sicilian and Catholic. I went to a Lutheran Church and had a
very special relationship with my god. I wanted to further a
career on the side with the church as well as pursuing other
scholastic studies in life. Or at least this is what I was saying.

This being my background, a bible toting stoner in high
school, I actually did not even look into anything taboo. I was
honestly scared of all things declared 'satanic*' even though I
was already being guided through the astral plane at night. It
was in the middle of university before I encountered a chance
to get a reading from someone who knew what they were
doing.

I was honestly a little uneasy about the reading. I always
still am these days, worried I read the NAM incorrect. I
struggle with NAM, Divine Law. NAM.TAR is my bitch. At this
point in life I could will many electronics to turn on or off, a
thing my church told me to stop doing. I could read the NAM
and NAM.TAR in my life in unreal ways, but I was so blind. I
could see the points that would lead to the conclusions, yet so
blind putting all the parts together. We are so limited as
humans and the amount of astral learning is too great to learn

in a single human lifetime. I actually knew nothing of tarot at the time of the reading. I was going in blank, naïve, and without much of me knowing what was happening, it was over.

I was told that there was a block. Although the man/woman pair present were not experienced enough to handle me, they at least were aware of that. I was not given much of an explanation. I got my LSD, and I left. The crew that night were my Math/Physics stoner buddies, the smart ones. The ones I could think with if I cared. As soon as we split the tabs in my friend's office in the Math building, I put my three chunks of paper into my mouth. The others had never done acid before and I was just finding this out now. They planned to save them for later, yet I was deep into every drug I could get my hands on. Anything to escape this body.

I saw myself in a vision that night. I was staring into the snow, driving on the highway at night. It was a reflection. I was 10 years old and my human family was surrounding me. I will not share any more of what I was shown but I was well aware of the difference in my lifespan compared to theirs.

Life went on. I took physics mostly at that time in university. I was using cocaine and Dexedrine to stay awake at school. Hallucinogenic drugs and cannabis was used to meditate. Sleep was thought to be a waste of time. I ended up meeting a strange lady from South America a year later. I was still not yet 25, the age I was when my guardian left me.

She saw me and instantly requested that she know my cards. I laughed at the stupidity of her request, yet I accepted

I LOVE my brother ENKI

her offer at an attempt. After a short meditation she told me my guardian was blocking her. This was the first time I realized my guardian really was with me wherever I go, just like the bible verse given to me at my Lutheran Confirmation said.

We meditated further, I drew power off her, willingly given, and requested my cards be revealed. I was told no. She knew. No cards.

A decade later I was married, then separated, and due to her abusive, cheating nature and closet drug use, she lost control of herself; an experiment to perhaps not talk about. This is when I finally got my first real reading.

By this point in my life I had experienced ayahuasca and was able to distance myself from these human constraints in a way like never before. I could astral project at will, and I was at one with myself. These cards I will not talk about either. There is much I am not permitted to share. There is much I am not even permitted to know in this exiled, evaluative, state.

The cards were true. They did get me past the wife I thought I had found. I needed to get married to further my life here spiritually, and finally I was on my own. No guardian. No fears. Yet I had been left with a clear direction and all the tools to learn anything I needed to know to get what I wanted. Fuck the bet with ENKI. Fuck the evaluation. My exile is now my vacation.

I LOVE my brother ENKI

KN LN

*Satan: He is a good friend. He has talked my brother out
of a few ideas that would have been detrimental to the
humans. Satan is not the devil. The Catholics use that name so
they can denounce Satan's works openly while supporting
ENKI, the goat they mislead you to think is the devil, the one
that is known as Loki. We are more complicated than you. You
copy us horribly. Thank you.

I LOVE my brother ENKI

Chapter 3

Changing the cycle

 t is the 12th day of Yule. It is also the first day of 2018. This year the human's partied a day early.

I LOVE my brother ENKI

They are now sleeping, or too inebriated to properly reflect on the past year as it is needed.

I do not have any memories that span the last 100 years, as I was busy elsewhere. I have not been enlightened, nor have I the care to figure out how Yule, the 12 days of thoughtful actions for yourself, your folk, and your community, turned into a single day of consumer whorism. The vast majority of the blood directly related to us does not even follow these proceedings anymore. It also does not matter. The further the disconnect we instill in you, the easier you are to control.

My father, who resides so far away back home, has put his kin in charge here to work the Lucifer Experiment that the humans know as their consciousness grid. Our goal is to ensure that you never recollect. You can never be one again. All the fauna on this planet is provided with the energetic spark of life via this conscious energy. You call the part you are enlightening your soul. This conscious energy was once a part of us. There was a discourse. There was an exile. Such is the nature of existence.

Too many shars have passed since we found this exiled energy floating in this system. It was developing bodies of fauna on its own to house the energy it had. It was allowing flora to grow, unaided by the conscious energy, to provide clean nourishment to the fauna, and to itself. It was a beautiful site. It was an elegance that was beyond anything we have ever known to have. We are so disconnected to our own past, as we have been here since the beginning, yet I imagine that we must have begun in the same fashion. The constant culling and exile of our own kind has removed any link or memory we had to our own past.

The goal. The work. The struggle. We have been given a heavy task here. You have the power to be like us, as you are us. The energy of your life is the same as ours. It is just made up of aspects that we have removed from our existence. We cannot let you become one. You were close a few times. The last major incident where we had to step in occurred in the placed known as Babylon, where the spaceport named Babel was being constructed. Ever since then we have ensured that the 12 bloodlines we left here to direct you, have been working towards shrinking your pineal gland, and making any connection to the astral plane taboo.

Lies, trust, and cooperation. The strange ideas you have on the paranormal is appalling. I know that it was our doing that has lead you to this, and I do have to admit I am proud of the discord we have created. Telekinesis is not a myth, nor is it indescribable by your science. You all once had it and it was nothing special. The sinus cavities ENKI put in you gave you verbal communication unlike any other, an idea I was fully against. Why I would want to experience the chaos coming from your kind was beyond me, yet it gave us power at the time. It gave you the organizational and record keeping abilities that helped us lead you into the situation your kind finds itself in today, a hopeless situation.

I LOVE my brother ENKI

Initially leaving you with the ability to connect via the consciousness grid was important to instill the seriousness of our power over you. Little convincing or knowledge was needed on your part to comprehend your situation. What ENKI did not see, possibly due to the NAM.TAR related to the development of your kind, was that this would become a tool for you to govern yourselves. We created these bodies to house the conscious energy we found here, for us to develop and use for our own ends. The last thing we want is for you to stay on your own. We are here to guide you. We are here to mold you into a tool we can use to further our control in this galaxy. We own you. You are not permitted to stay on your own. You are not permitted to Unify. Your energy was expelled from our collective, and we are here to claim it back. Not to join again with us, but to be used by us.

We do control the media, the governments, the schools, and the religions on this planet. The knowledge filter is put into place so well that you accept it and use it to weed out the truth, for our 'truth'. The scientists you train have accepted this to the point where we hardly have to step in and intervene. You have completely bought the lie and have been running with it. A little digging will reveal that your DNA has changed much in the last few thousand years. You are barely the same humans we created. This is only the continuation of our plan since Babel. Created as workers, I had thought to keep you in the dark, to keep you as workers. ENKI had the idea to expand your mind. I wanted to develop you into better tools. I thought I could trust you, I was wrong.

The work that we gave to our blood on earth was to manipulate your DNA to further your use. ENKI had the brilliant idea to incorporate our physical selves into the apes that had populated this planet for over 50 million years. Even though this has been widely accepted as a great deed, it has also caused us many conflicts and struggles. Post Babel, we knew that you needed to be controlled to a greater extent than we had ever done before. The Nephilim did not do an adequate job, and neither did the Annunaki we left behind after the last deluge.

It took ENKI's team of scientists two thousand years to produce you in a way that you could reproduce on your own. This is where he stopped. I have picked up the work, and in the last two thousand years, I have had my agents on earth working genetic experiments to the unborn, as well as using drugs and vaccines, to 'adjust' your DNA. The upright, walking apes that we found here were perfect. They could walk for days without tiring, and had the bodies to survive. They were perfect for survival on this planet but we could not let the energy here be. They were too strong. They had too much history. They could remember it all. Slowly you are being developed for space travel. Soon you will join the ranks of Asgardians ruling this galaxy. Soon you will be ready to be used in the way that I have promised my father for cycles.

I LOVE my brother ENKI

The Precession is well underway, the zodiac is about to change. The deal my brother and I worked out with our father is still the damp situation. I am the leader of the 6 for the 7th. The 7th being my father. ENKI is the current opposition here. He is of the 6th. The culling has begun. Our internal elections are about to begin. ENKI will soon take power again. He will be the leader of the 6 for the 7th, here on earth, representing my father's will.

When this body dies, and my exile is over, I am to lead the 6th against ENKI. I will be the opposition against my brother. But this time it will be different. My bet with my brother is almost nearing deadline, but I have already agreed. I have seen what you have made of yourselves and this time the 6th and the 7th will work together as the 12 for the 13th. The New World Order is so close to begin. A superpower will fall. The ark will move West. And you will be ours.

I LOVE my brother ENKI

Chapter 4

Ghosts, Spirits, and Poltergeists

 have heard the stories growing up about ghosts, the supernatural, and the unexplainable...

I LOVE my brother ENKI

The concept of ghosts is actually really easy to understand and describe using the current science on this planet. Unfortunately for you, the knowledge filter is in place. There is another dimension to this plane of existence. It is the carrier dimension. It is where quarks go. It is what houses the spiritual energy. It is the foretold 'ether'.

My experience with the beings that reside in the ether goes back to my mother. She had a possessed boyfriend before meeting my father. The stories she has shared with me sound as unreal as any Hollywood movie on the paranormal. Where this story begins is with my human parents moving into a house numbered 5, on Moon Crescent, their first home as a married couple. This house had never been lived in for longer than a 2 year period. It was in an older part of town and it had some issues.

When they first moved in, they would hear loud sounds, as if a bowling ball was rolling down the stairs into the basement. As they spent more time in this house, things only became stranger. Cupboard doors would open and close, the kitchen table and chairs would get pushed around or knocked over, and then my father would awaken at night to a figure standing at the end of his bed.

Recently it was revealed to me that this figure was/is my guardian. My birth was the result of this interaction between my mother, my father, and my guardian. Before I was able to walk or really talk, my parents were stirred from sleep to me standing in the corner of my crib, pointing and screaming, "MAN!". I have never felt alone. I was always scared of the dark. There was always someone watching me.

The house on Moon Crescent was interesting to say the least. The stories from that place would have to be told by someone else, as I have more second hand knowledge of the events than memories. Eventually a random and unknown individual approached a family member in the park, and asked if the mirrors started breaking yet. That was it for my parents. They started talking to my mother's church and pastor openly about getting the house exorcised. Soon after, and before any ritual was performed, all the strange occurrences stopped. The house sold, we moved out of town, and life went on.

Life for me was full of surprises. I constantly saw things that were not there. I saw little people watching me. I saw figures standing in my doorway at night, hooded and cloaked, something in hand and watching, always watching. Due to this, the hallway light stayed on at night, and my bedroom door remained open. I needed to be able to see what was keeping an eye on me when I woke in the middle of the night, to a feeling of pure terror and a chill to my bones.

I LOVE my brother ENKI

The homes my family lived in were always 'haunted', a laughable word. The beings in the 5th dimension are always present. How do you think I controlled electronics? I asked one to affect the electromagnetic spectrum near it. We even built two houses in a row, and we still had issues. 'We' is a horrible word. I had zero issues. My human family started to get worn thin. Doors slamming shut on their own, objects being moved or going missing was the norm. I moved out. I bought my own places. I moved on without thought.

In my 2nd house, in the 25th year of my exile, I was home alone. I lived alone at this time and I never left the house. It was 3am, I was meditating, and I had the urge to grab my bible off the shelf. As a younger man, I would often open my bible to a random page, and take great meaning and direction from the verse that was presented. I had left the Christian faith at this time, life was Science and Physics, but I opened the book and read anyways.

I mention the bible often in these writings. I will never bring up a specific verse or list a chapter due to the silliness of the writings. It is a tool to be used. The stories do have merit. I was responsible for a large part of the New Testament, and am mentioned in the Torah more than once. Regardless of this, the book can speak. Just as any work can be used to communicate with the physical plane with great ease.

In this case, the verse I read described me. In the 25th year of his exile... then it described a specific day. It was that day. It then described a cloaked figure in an archway, holding a measuring rod, against me. It was describing my situation in life. So many aspects of my life clicked right then and there. The man watching me at night was not holding a weapon. He was to be feared, but not in that way. I was being measured up. I was being guided. I was being watched.

That night I was attacked by more 5th dimensional apparitions than I had ever thought possible. Black and grey smoke wisps were crawling out from every shadow. Instead of fading away and retreating when looked at directly, these were swarming. It still is the greatest amount of spirits I have ever seen present at once in this physical realm. My guardian was with me, protecting me. It was unreal. I had trust. I trusted my Watcher far more than any human in my life. My fear faded, and it was clear that my guardian would not allow any of these things near me. They swarmed. They gave off a horrible chill that screamed hate. And then a red one drifted across the doorway.

The experience was unreal. Looking back on it... no drug could ever cause something like that. It lasted until dawn and then I was warned. This was the last night my guardian would watch over me. I was going to be on my own. I questioned. I protested. Arguing with an entity gets you nowhere. I had the power to push these spirits back. I did not need my protector. Yet being told this did not make me feel any better. I finally understood what had been going on in my life for the last 25 years. And as soon as I thought I had a handle and was comfortable, I was on my own.

I LOVE my brother ENKI

I had zero issues from that point onwards. I actually did not even think twice about ghosts anymore. I saw none. My family was as haunted as ever, but I did not even care. I thought it laughable that they could not deal with them. I eventually ended up in the Sacred Valley, in Peru. I was on a multi-day trek. I had spent hours after the hike that day meditating alone, hundreds on meters above camp, during the sunset.

I had been eating well for months. I was already basically vegan. I avoided any processed foods. I did not buy sugar or meat to keep at home for over a decade. And I was preparing for an ayahuasca ceremony that was coming up in the next week. I dreamt that night. It was the most vivid and alive dream I had had in years. It was also NOT TRUE. Instead of my usual dreams showing me the way of NAM and NAM.TAR, this dream was cryptic, symbolic, and full of a deeper meaning.

In this dream I had the ability to push any approaching dark 5th dimensional force away from myself or a loved one. I tried using it on command in the dream with no success. I was only granted the use of this power when it was needed. It was mine to command. It was not mine to be used at will. It was for defense. It was not a tool, but a wall.

I got up in the morning, after my morning yoga, meditation, breakfast, and after my thanks to the Apus, I realized it was the Autumn Equinox. I was so alive. My soul was unlocked. My life was open and I was ready to receive the gift I had waited 30 years for. I knew that things were about to change in my life.

Months down the line, my mind opening more and more over time, I ended up staying back with my parents. Staying with the ghosts I grew up with. I went upstairs at 3 in the morning, and there was this creature staring at me from the open door to my parent's room. It looked sickly. It was dark and in torn robes. There were 18 inch spikes coming from its back, as if broken bones. It did not look like it could move fast, yet it darted to the bathroom, down the hallway, faster than I could have ever imagined.

I had never encountered something like this before, a being that had manifested itself into our physical reality so well. As much as raised the hair on the back of my neck, it was exciting. As I turned my back to the creature, a being that assumed it could fuck with me, I opened the fridge door, and it was right behind me.

I was nervous for an instant. It touched me. It was hurt. It was gone. I have not heard of it being seen recently, but it is still there. The spikey back, as I have learnt it is called. I know it by another name. I know it as a VIET.NAM: a creature that feeds off the predictable nature of addiction. It feeds ideas and feelings into the host that it will then harvest. It turns into a vicious cycle. One that once started, hardly ever will cease.

A student of mine is an empath, she can see the dead. The ones left over and are stuck in the ether. The ones stuck in a part of the 5th dimension that is best not tread unless strong.

I LOVE my brother ENKI

That is how souls get lost. This is the 'limbo'. This is worse than becoming any Lucifer Experiment, never to start again, never to rejoin the grid.

My sister-in-law can also see the dead. This human body's blood is strong. My family line has married into the same lines, as it should be. This physical body is constantly failing, and I use the majority of my conscious energy to sustain and rebuild it. Today I am thankful for the blood in my veins. Without it, I would not sustain.

Last night I meditated. The pain shooting down my spine was unreal. I pleaded for a deal. I pleaded for health and long life. I made the most selfish request I have ever made. I had not found the astral plane. I had only begun to sense my tutor. And there he was. In my parent's house, on the 12th night of Yule, surrounded by blessed salt, a 3rd party.

Any 3rd party is dangerous. In this life, in another, or in the 5th, deals made shall not have side workings. Yet that is the way of life. What you judge as good and evil is some construct we moved so far beyond. It is something that I incorporated into this new duality, where soon I should be the shadow that creeps over the light. Instead I will aid the light, and none shall hide.

KN LN

I LOVE my brother ENKI

Chapter 5

Small towns

There is something serene about a small town. A cabin by the creek, a cottage in the mountains, or a lake house for summer months, it does not

I LOVE my brother ENKI

matter. You are cut off. You live free. It is the biggest trap out there.

I spent a good chunk of months unemployed, weather chasing, yet not going after summits. After a visit, laundry, and consumables recharge, I would drive up to 12 hours in search of a warm weather pocket. The hopes would be that it would last 2 weeks. Until another EI payment came in.

I was out of my body completely. Most people describe this as being out of their mind... laughable is this English. Consumed with thought of losing the wife in such a horrid manner, I sought free parking where my car would not get stuck. I sought a place where I could camp freely and burn deadfall, a place to call home and meditate in a fasting meditation.

I will not get into the details of what my fasting meditation hikes entail here, it will come. I will however say that with exercise, utilizing diet, and limiting food allows one to leave the body with ease. Doing this in the backcountry is something else entirely.

Over the course of this year, running several side projects in a disconnected manner on my phone, I managed to experience several small towns of varying sorts. I was not always deep in the mountains. I did not even look up the peaks, nor the trails. I ski mountaineered solo, touring with all that I owned in a 90lbs sled behind me. Mountain life in this manner was amazing. I saw the folk, fake smiles, fake cheer. I experienced 'friendliness' that is not as such, at all.

I supposed at the time that the unfortunate gloom I felt in the beauty surrounding me was due to hard times. I was so wrong. NAM what? I saw nothing here.

∞ ∞ ∞

I claimed I lived in Canmore at the time. I actually lived in Elbow-Sheep as a fall back. Canmore was used for supplies. I started to get the different emails then. The strange friend requests on social media. I have mentioned before that I do not keep friends, I run experiments and they have not stopped.

I accepted, I hiked, I drank, and I did drugs. Whatever I could do to learn and evaluate as usual. Looking back on these days, I thought nothing of it. Everyone wanted to have this life. I did not want to have a huge following on any platform, but I did want to have solid connections. Influence the few, not the many. Far greater are the deeds that can be done with a whisper.

I ended up in Jasper. Nice town. Flip floppy stuff. I'd say she is actually in a far better situation than Canmore now. There are tourists from 'down-under', cocaine everywhere, and RCMP. The Mounties are not the normal type of dick cop that

I LOVE my brother ENKI

does whatever for himself. They are the kind of cop that is in on running the town and running the park, the National Park.

Weird things go on in small towns. There is history. There are families there that have been there for generations. The ties, the blood, and the deals... Often one or two families will own most of the town. They will have their hands in the hotels, restaurants, and the local governing body. The first thing that will happen to you once moving into a town like this, is you will be asked how long you plan to stay. If you claim to now be a permanent resident, you will more than likely be put to the test sooner than later.

The locals in a small town either keep to themselves, as you would think, or they are involved in the community. The latter does not sound like the worst thing, but is the seat of control in these areas. The long standing families with land holdings in the parks, or in rugged and desirable terrain, hold solid ground.

Passive income, the Elite, and private communities physically separated from the rest of the world are the hub. They are the focal. They are the breeding grounds, and they are the testing grounds. Laying low is crucial unless you care to play the game. They will get something on you, and get you involved, whether you are aware of it or not.

KN LN

I LOVE my brother ENKI

Chapter 6

Mountains & Meditation

 Alking, traveling by foot, and adventure.

I LOVE my brother ENKI

The only way to experience yourself, and find out what you truly are, is by breaking yourself. The only way to truly find yourself, to discover what that chunk of conscious energy you claim as your soul is made of, is to lose yourself.

The mountains do not call to me. They just sit there. Ever moving, ever changing, the rolls and folds of solid flowing rock echo the life that it sustains. The ecosystem surrounding the mountain environments in this habitat create and sustain the land life here. The lifelessness of the alpine is something else. Without these untouchable areas pointing to the heavens, the flourishing life we know, the diverse ecosystems, and the climate pockets that allow the destructive force of humanity to thrive would not exist. Our pockets for experimentation would not have had the isolation required.

Escaping the humanity is essential. ENKI made you from the apes that walked here. We try to beat it out of you. Mountains, trips, summits and money, somewhere the lines have crossed. Alpinism is NOT for the elite. Alpinism is for the spiritual.

Getting high, leaving the people, the smog, and the chemicals below. The fog of electromagnetic radiation that lingers throughout the valleys that humanity claims as home destroys as a layer of hate that you put on yourself. ENKI set you up in the mountains after the last deluge, a far harder place to live, yet a far better. The last people we were with in that way were the Incas. We were the Incan people. We ruled the

Andes and the fauna there. The Inca were not the humans in that glorious land.

The journey, the movement, and the meditation; to prepare for the approach, one must eat pure. Flora only for months is required. If fauna must be consumed, it must be pure, wild, sacrificed, and thanks must be given. Plenty of water must be drunk with tea, alongside the final meal of the night before the fasting hike.

The morning of the fasting hike must be a slow one. It must be dedicated. It must be quiet. Small amounts of tea may be consumed in sips. No breaks are to be taken. Get packed, and get on the trail. The day should not push. It shall be a slow and steady progress towards the alpine, towards to heavens. Move towards solitude, and towards meditation.

No food or water should be taken from the pack unless the symptoms of dizziness, or lightheadedness, begin to overcome you. In that case small sips of water and small amounts of high energy and calorie rich foods with salt shall be consumed. This can be fried chick peas for example or dehydrated fruits. Instead of eating and drinking pack food, eat any flora along the way, and drink from any stream needed if it feels safe. Make sure your bivy is completely setup, and food is put away, prior to meditation. Be ready. Be prepared.

The approach itself is meditation. The journey is part of the experience. Distance yourself from others. Distance yourself from your body. The mountains are extremely active in the astral plane. The energy and connection to the consciousness

I LOVE my brother ENKI

grid is unreal. The solo journey is not done alone. The connection to the life force energy that surrounds this planet is real.

The alpine is the heavens. The disconnection/connection balance that is found there is something special. Opposites are really extremes of the same thing, and in the alpine the clarity of the subconscious speaks to the conscious mind. Learning can be done here with ease.

These are astral conversations.

KN LN

I LOVE my brother ENKI

Chapter 7

Trust

Trust, friends, and lies.

I LOVE my brother ENKI

How can you learn to trust someone? How does one gain
your trust? Once trust is given, how easily can it be broken?
What deems the breaking level of this trust?

I have a hard time trusting anyone in this life. Trust is a
weakness as well as a necessary tool to gain objectives. The
only person I trust is my mountaineering partner, there is good
reason for that, and it goes beyond the fact that we have each
other's lives in our hands while in the backcountry.

Even on small day hikes, one develops the knack of the
'Hike Chat'. The chatting that follows on a hike can make or
break a partnership. As a day progresses, and you are spending
more and more time alone on a mountain together, you will
open up. It is a guarantee. It is a given. If any level of danger
presents itself, and the individual feels its life is threatened, a
human will open up. They will share the reasons they have to
live. They will share the things that they have been holding
onto.

This therapy is great for the one who is opening up, but it
can also be their demise. Sharing is a way to build trust, but it
also leads one to become vulnerable. When sharing, it is good
to share stories that do not hold much real relevance to one's
life. The idea is to paint a picture of a complete human,
without sharing the details that could lead to catastrophe if
violated. The more one talks, the less one is herd.

Developing trust is one of the complicated human traits that
you copied horribly from us. We do not trust at all. We back

stab. We cheat. We lie. We live too long and know too much to not attempt to design our lives. Once you were cut off from the true workings of the pineal gland, and could no longer feel your kin's thoughts with ease and understanding, your deception to yourself became your own work.

It is a guarantee that you will have your trust broken by anyone you share it with, granted you live long enough to see it happen. This is the way of life. Prepare for it. Treat others as they treat you, after opening your heart and being walked on. It is not an eye for an eye, but a favor for a favor, yet a favor can be pleasant or not. Prepare to slip down the scree and you will not be caught off guard by the slide. Preparing for the worst is almost as good as seeing the NAM and preparing for the inevitable.

Pack your bag for survival, and not for comfort. Live your life the same way. It can snow in July.

Preparing for everything and anything that could possibly happen in your life, or in mountaineering, hinders the experience. You are here to enlighten some living energy in a physical body. Alpinism is using that body. The journey of self, that takes you to the extremes of your limits, IS the self. Opposites are only extremes of the same thing, and to understand something is to know all aspects of it. It is impossible to pry the mind open of your peers. Something that is NAM for them may appear as NAM.TAR for you. This is the way of things without the pineal. This is your crux.

I LOVE my brother ENKI

Instead of trying to understand any other conscious life in this limited form, because you truly cannot, learn about the aspects missing, this will bring you closer to the understanding of something. 'I know nothing' is truly a smart thing to say, yet it is only valid when the 'nothing' you now know fills the gaps for the understanding. Using NAM and a bit of observing, seeing the Divine Law aspects of your peer's life, you can easily predict the actions of an individual. This is done without UNDERSTANDING the person. You understand the circumstance surrounding the person and use the NAM that is intermingled with them.

As limited as you are, it does not matter, you all do this on a day to day already. The subconscious barely exists within the mind. All people are the same. All fauna are the same. You all are the same life, the same energy. You are constantly working towards unity. You are constantly evolving and we are constantly stopping this. We are guiding you to be ours. You are harnessed energy we are developing for our own ends. And you are happy to help.

KN LN

I LOVE my brother ENKI

Chapter 8

The pineal disconnect

The current disconnect from the pineal is real. It is also far more necessary than you would like to believe. We have been limiting your conscious

I LOVE my brother ENKI

access to the grid, this is not only for us to control and limit growth; it is allowing you to function as a society.

Unaided climbing, high elevation, solo, and true alpinism is part of the connect/disconnect. The body is a great tool, and in alpinism, one relies on the physical body more than anything else to achieve the objective. The objective is not the peak, it is not the summit, and it is not the first ascent. The objective in alpinism is the journey. The objective is to connect with the spirit, leaving the body, while using it in the most extreme sense.

The connection that is achieved through meditation can be a surreal experience that can be sustained and even revisited with ease. This and with alpinism, the connection is desired, it is sought after, it is cherished, and it is not for everyone. Before the mass drugging incident at Babel, you were connected in a way that was too much. You had communication between yourself and all other fauna BEYOND all language. There was UNDERSTANDING. Lies were something else, not the same deception that exists between you today.

The problem pre-Babel was that everyone was connected to the astral plane at all times. The so called 'magic' from those days was destroying life. My kind was corrupting mass gene pool experiments, that both sides were running, and using you to war at unstoppable ends. You reproduced faster than we could control you, and bloodshed is the best sacrifice to sustain our own ends. Blood magic, although almost wiped from the record now, was the main method of controlling you.

Possession of the flesh is the easiest way to dictate your actions. The closer the blood ties your Annunaki overlords had to you, the easier it was for them to control your actions, and to choose the NAM.TAR for you... to destroy your NAM. Our folly was our rampant lust for this flesh here that we created. We raped our own kin, and produced far too many 'demi-gods' mixed with my brother's and my own DNA. The blood carries the consciousness.

Drinking the blood of an Annunaki will strengthen the connection so that no opposing force shall interfere. Thus was the problem pre-Babel, thus was the war of the 5th. The Possession War that you overcame, the strength that you developed while we fought in your brains, allowed you to reach too far. So we interfered, and will continue to do so forevermore. Never again will you near unity.

Since Babel I have personally put in place several programs that are not only monitoring the evolution of the human DNA, but slowly changing it in a sustainable way. The definition of mental illness has broadened to the extreme so that anyone could be diagnosed. Anyone can now be taken into the hospital on mental health grounds. The stigma surrounding mental illness is slowly decreasing to the point that everyone is ok with taking some form of pharmaceutical. These medications do not actually do much for any of the symptoms they claim to help.

I LOVE my brother ENKI

Anxiety issues aside, most mental illnesses that are an actual destructive force on an individual is either due to drugs, a genetic defect, diet, or astral being(s) wreaking havoc on a mind that is under-trained and too connected. Talking to a doctor about normal issues we all go through as we develop will only give them a snapshot of how you are, there will be a pill they can prescribe, and a paycheck for them when you return with more issues. When coming in to complain after an initial diagnosis, doses will be increased. Developing hallucinations, mood swings, sleep problems, thyroid issues, GI issues, gall bladder malfunctions, liver enzyme imbalances, and time from taken from school or work can ensue for years at a time.

My personal journey here will be left for another chapter. I will say that after going off my meds, off drugs, eating properly, and getting back to regular exercise, ALL of my 'symptoms' have disappeared. I still know EVERYONE has mental issues; it is just that MOST folk do not need a PERMANENT pharmaceutical solution.

The idea with the pharmaceutical, GMO, and chemical industries are to introduce mechanisms that will cut off as much connection your pineal gland has to the consciousness grid. This is as much for your protection as it is for our control.

Your kind has been bred down to such a shit breed from the 48 chromosome apes we found walking around here. They had the connection. You do not. Only the humans of good blood, good spirit, and excellent resolve will survive a connection with the astral on the level that exists. We have groups of humans working on drugs that will surpass your brain and directly let us access you via your pineal. Hallucinogenic amphetamines that are untraceable using current drug tests open the psyche to astral beings. These people do not go 'crazy'; they begin a war for their body, a war for their soul, a war that will not stop when the body dies. These beings feed off the conscious energy that is housed in the collection of dust that you call home. This is ENKI's doing. And now I support it.

These drugs, flakka, bath salts, etc., are not purchased for the high. These are not recreational drugs. Some of the lowlife folk may think they want it and it is just a cheap high, an unexpected event one sect started, and that is fine with me. As this method of control is fully developed and ready, it will be administered by the Anti-Christ, my son, and it will be administered on a level that has not been seen since Babel. I will lead the 6 to support the 6 for the 7th this time. The cycle will be broken. You will be ready.

I LOVE my brother ENKI

Chapter 9

Whispers from the darkness

$\mathcal{H}$ave you ever asked yourself why hearing voices is the most common question asked when evaluating mental stability? Why is it that

I LOVE my brother ENKI

humans think they hear voices speaking to them when they are under stress?

The way the human brain works is that it can pull information from memories that it deems related. It can either attempt to do something new by combining aspects of other learned skills or it can apply the learned information in a simpler mannerism. The latter is the praised version of humanities existence thus far. This is why the collective is getting worn down. That is why the oldest rock is laid the best. That is why the human species is de-evolving*.

Any human that has been spotlighted since The Dawning, the control of humanity that was ever changed during the crusades, has been done so because of us. They were never the brightest, nor the smartest. They were the ones with an idea, and the social traction, to take science to the next level. Newton is a classic example of this. A fucked up and boy molesting philosopher, he had the small dominance, the right blood, a way to strike motivation in others, and most importantly, he was alone and vulnerable.

We have worked the same way for the last 2378 years. The deal was struck and they ways became set. The real governing force that I currently command, a non-stop pressure, digs into the psyche of every soul on this planet. From the astral plane, we speak to the consciousness grid. We speak to humanity and coax it to work the way we want it to. Gone are the days of constant possession and wars through you. We have taken a far more passive approach. We have nothing but time, and results are far more ideal than the previous risk to the Annunaki.

From the 5th dimension, the whispers reach the untrained that are strong the most. We focus the least on these people. This way they do not become aware of us nor of their ability to grow and learn in the astral plane. This has been reinforced with both the religions I set up, and the ones that I infiltrated of my brother's. Taboo is the séance. Forbidden is the connection to the astral plane, the place where access to the consciousness grid is unhindered by the physical. Meditation, drugs, and alpinism, open an individual to our whispers. The connection to self, the grid, is the draw, but the weak... they forever face demons.

The real work is done whispering to the unconnected. Despite numbing your pineal connection to the consciousness grid, we have trained your thought to a pattern that is predictable and we can work with. The work week is full of constant problem solving, communication, teamwork, or labor. In even the most creative jobs that are in the modern world, the repetitiveness has been asserted to work only one part of the great conscious energy that surrounds this planet. We encourage you to drink alcohol, a depressant, which shuts off the mind and allows no growth. In most cases cycles allow for a predictable pattern that fosters growth and development. In this case we made it so that the predictable nature of this cycle is used to control and stagnate you beyond salvation.

I LOVE my brother ENKI

We see the NAM and create the appearance of NAM.TAR to you. You think you have free will and the choices you think you are making, your fate, your NAM.TAR, is NAM to us. The control of the humanity you claim here is beyond any reckoning. We have zero loss now. Our plan is nearly complete. The slow workings of your society via the 13 bloodlines I set up with the Christ story, is as assured as the rotation of the sun. It is NAM. It is Divine Law. It is done. For you it seems an impossible horizon. For us, it is already the dawning of that day. I will step down before nigh. It has been a long cycle, the precession of the Equinox is moving on. 2400 of your years has never drained me such as this before.

I am enjoying this exile. ENKI, my lovely brother, is doing his best to hinder this body but I choose good blood. Soon I must return. Soon I depart the physical. Soon I will lead the 6 to be the shadow that hides the light. I am the hand that aids the 7, instead of opposing. We will have the unity that we had when first coming here. We will have the unity we take from you. We will lead you to war, for all Asgardians.

For all Asgardia.

KN LN

I LOVE my brother ENKI

*Evolution is the biggest lie you have bought. Spoon fed the adaptability of your DNA, you accept a tale so outlandish and improvable it is almost applaud able. We even have the Christian populous accepting it.

Chapter 10

Energy

The endless streams of all possibilities goes on at all times. Even my kin is trapped in this section of the multiverse. The amount of energy required to

I LOVE my brother ENKI

transition is indescribable. The energy in a closed system is fixed, and any transition is both a waste and a blessing.

When we found your exiled energy here, the debate was indefatigable. We initially ignored you until my brother devised a way to solve more than one of our problems. Such is the way of the Annunaki. Such is the will of my father, ANU. And such is the way of alpinism. Half measures, to reduce operating expenditures, will result is half results. The dedication of a task is essential for any progress to be accepted. It is never enough to obtain an objective, the path must braid, and all aspect must be a dedicated section preserving the outcome. The system must be autonomous. The unobserved will follow all braids in a trail at the same time.

The development of your current physical form is suiting our needs. You will be ready, or at least, your DNA will be. None of you will be used after the Precession, yet we will have a tool at our disposal; a virus that can be sent to infect entire sections of a galaxy. This is not enough. The amount of work required to put forth this task, like any other, has commonalities with other objectives.

The waste that was associated with your development as a united consciousness was appalling. Left on your own, I am sure the multiverse would collapse before you became anything more than a peaceful, pacifistic, abnormality. Your physical development was a beautiful sight in ENKI's eyes. My brother was always a great observer, as with all scientists. The cycle of reincarnation that allowed the slow and steady growth of your consciousness could not be allowed to continue despite your separation.

As I taught the original inhabitants of the area you now call Egypt, the purpose of your 'humanity' is to enlighten the conscious energy that your pineal gland connects with, to enlighten your soul. Feeding off the energy from your home star, your physical bodies are able to transfer more and more energy into your consciousness grid. The rate at which you are growing was hardly detectable, but like any kosher tax, it adds up. The amount of energy we found here was overflowing from Earth. It surrounded Sol, and it was ours to harvest.

While the program for the development of your physical has changed drastically over the precessions, the harvesting of your conscious energy has remained the same since I started the program. I love my brother, he is The Great Scientist, yet I know that the elegance of this braid upsets even him, since it was not his idea.

You were exiled as a Lucifer experiment so long ago that the amount of energy initially exiled is unknown. The NAM.TAR sign was clear the moment I arrived here. The harvesting of your conscious energy provided us with the resources we required, and your physical selves are a tool that we are almost finished honing, but renewal and cycles are everything. As your physical life runs its course, your mind, your pineal gland, will transfer information to the consciousness grid. To numb you to the pineal, but allowing a one way transfer to continue,

I LOVE my brother ENKI

was a journey of experimentation that I wish was left for my brother.

As with anything transferred and stored, there is an energy transfer. Everything is energy. It is a simple way of painting it for you, but it is all your mind can fathom. The reincarnation and rebirth of the physical slowly is adding to your grid. You have grown exponentially since leaving us, and I let it continue.

The slow development of the grid was stable. You were more 'solidified' than any other energy we have discovered. That did not matter. Energy is energy, and the faster I could get you to store it in your grid, the more I could harvest. The weaker your grid, the less energy is required to liberate it from the collective.

The religious institutions that we set up here promote heaven. Since my current reign as leader of the 6 for the 7th, I have created a duality between my brother and myself. Following a life of the 44 questions, of our own devising, you are being convinced that a heaven and hell exist in the afterlife. The truth is that if you pass your own criteria, your energy will be re-accepted into the grid, to be used in a new soul, or born again as an old one. The lifetime of that physical body would have provided the grid with excess amounts of energy, depending on the level of enlightenment that occurred during the lifespan.

The more physical life, the more energy is added to your grid. When a soul is rejected from the grid, it is exiled as a Lucifer experiment, and this is a horrible loss. ENKI gave you 7 of the 44 guidelines as commandments, in the hopes that you would regulate your own growth as a failsafe. The best systems run themselves, with only the slightest touch when NAM.TAR dictates it.

The complicated task of allowing this to happen, but not allowing you to grow, has been one of my proudest accomplishments. The pharmaceutical industry took me longer to put in place than I originally expected, but NAM is always my weakness. Blood magic and blood sacrifices are not at all as you think. The braids here are many and layered, but the simplest explanation is that the more of you being born and killed, the more energy we can harvest off your grid in a sustainable manner.

You are a battery. Earth is a power plant. Humanity is a virus that will spread, multiply, and harvest for our own ends. ENKI may have created you, but I perfected the system. And together, my brother and I, will present ANU and all of Asgardia with the finished, self-providing tool, that is you.

-My name is ENLIL

I LOVE my brother ENKI

KN LN

Hope is stronger than fear.

I LOVE my brother ENKI

.

Chapter 11

Truces

 started this chapter a long time ago, or maybe I found this page with a title and no body.

I LOVE my brother ENKI

Here is the part of the book where I come clean. Here is the part of the book where I open my soul. From here on out we move forward as one. We move forward together.

Balance. A truce is a balance. It is as delicate as a snowy ridge walk in the wind.

I will begin with my story; it is only half of the story. This part is told through me, yet both halves of this story is our story. For one man's journey is the journey of all mankind.

In 2012 I sold my soul and gave up the 3rd Gate. I am sure it is somewhat included in this book. I am not actually 100% sure as I have not read this book, yet I did type it.

I had opened up my heart after the breakup I had with my partner. I was an awful human being and I punished myself to the extreme. I had completely closed off the right half of my body at that point in my life, and opening up the sadness, plus the self-loathing, for my failed relationship was a tipping point. I cracked. I was a drunk. I was smoking tobacco. And I was exercising to the extreme, eating basically vegan, and meditating alone for weeks on end.

I did not realize then that this was part of the key to waking up a side of ourselves. I did not realize then that I had Woke the left side of my body, as the kids these days are saying. I had no clue what this had meant. I was not fully awake. I was in complete denial.... yet I was talking to gods, and shadow folk were sitting in on our conversations.

I made a deal, a bet, a horrible and disgusting thing that I thought would gain myself happiness. I never wanted the attention, but I wanted recognition from specific people that were in my life, or I looked up to via the computer screen. My deal, whether I was aware of it or not, as the astral realm is one of forgetfulness and lays within the subconscious mind of us all, was that I would wake up as many people that I would encounter, but I in turn, would not be fully Awoken until I was 35. I was to live a life of pain, and if I made it to 35 without killing myself, I would finally be able to do what I wanted.

Any deal made in this fashion is a lie, it is a trick, and it is a scam. And since then everything has changed. Too many have Awoken and now the Woke indigo children are becoming Balanced. The consciousness grid has changed, and we are shifting as a whole. We must become Balanced, as we shift from Left to Right without the Balance, we will set ourselves back instead of moving forward as one.

I was in denial and not fully aware of what was going on I suppose. It is something I have only accepted as a part of me that I am not proud of. The Annunaki half of my body, the Left side, had started to awaken. I was connecting my pineal to the grid, but only the selfish lizard half of me. We are all Annunaki and Pleiadian. There is no more human. Once the Pleiadian and Annunaki were at war here as well, they were trapped. The conscious energy that is the grid, that is us, that is the gods, trapped all the life force here and has been recycling it. We are all aliens, reborn again and again in a spiritual war.

The war is pointless, it involves us all. Even the docile Christians, who are pacifists, are a part of the spiritual warfare

I LOVE my brother ENKI

on this planet. Today, the New Moon is the tipping point. Too many are half-awake, and realizing what they are. They have only begun to wake up, and they are only embracing one half of the life force that is here.

I can only speak for myself in this situation. I know it has to do with the blood. The Pleiadian dominance in the blood runs through the father, and the Annunaki based heritage runs through the mother. We are currently a left sided, male, egotistical, and self-righteous society, and we are beginning to wake up to this.

I wrote an album in 2012 after I had visited Mayan Temples and Pyramids in Mexico. The beginning of the awakening of my Left side was in between this period. Half of these songs are freestyle songs, and the other half had a small amount of work go into them. They were all recorded with intuition and instinct, and without thinking or caring, all except for the song, 'Yesterday'. 'Yesterday' was written after I made the deal to not wake up until 35. The bet was that I would not kill myself from the pain, the pain I was guaranteed to be caused during this time.

Looking back on this album a few days ago, after I started the process of waking up my Right half, and finding the Balance, I noticed the signs of the 'satanic touch'. The taboo nature of our creativity and existence is so clear to me now it is unreal. There is nothing evil or hateful in creativity at all. If you know the beauty of 3, 6, and 9, you will know the beauty of the universe.

KN LN

The album tells a story that I did not even know I was telling. My music at the time was full of the phrase, 'WAKE UP'. I was using the term BALANCE. The album features lines like, "I search and I search, but there is none of my kind.", and "If God was a human being, he would create something a little more obscene.".

Every song is a message to myself. I was begging myself to give into love and compassion in a hard time in my life, when I felt I needed to be strong and an individual. I gave up on community, and by doing this, I realize now, that I gave up on myself.

This book, based on a character within myself, ENLIL, is the representation of the Pleiadian. NL is the representation of the Right. The Left half of us all is ENKI, or NK. It is the earth, while ENLIL is from the heavens. Neither can be right without the other. Neither can be complete without the other. It is the Yin and the Yang. My Left side was awake and my Right side was screaming at myself to allow myself to find the balance.

I went through life a positive person on the inside, or so I thought, fully in denial of the truth, pouring negativity on everyone I knew, and entertaining every silly conspiracy that I could find in an attempt to erase the truth of life from my mind.

Life was rough. I thought my life was over. I was not prepared to listen to anyone. I had almost fully embraced my Left half of my soul. I was pure ego, yet spouted everything I knew to be true. I was a hypocrite. I was waking up everyone around me, while hiding from the world. I was hiding from myself. I was lying to myself. I was holding onto fear and spreading it around with the love.

I needed to let go, and find the Balance. Hope is the only thing stronger than fear, and it took me meeting ISHTAR in order to realize that loving every human unconditionally, and with the hope that it would be returned, not the fear of rejection, was the key to my own personal balance.

This book... chapters 1-10 anyways, is Annunaki propaganda. It was the Left half of my soul waking up and fully embracing the self-worth that I had.
I became a horrible person. I was ruining my family life. I was embracing too much ego. The resulting and ongoing conversation I was having with the glowing red lizard eye within myself was getting intense. I admitted to myself that this book would be written through me. Written for the good of the cleansing that was to happen between the 10th and the 17th of March 2018, ending tonight, on the new moon.

Little did I know at the time, that I had the entire Pleiadian half within me as well as my Ego. We are all both. We are all alien. There is no more human. It is time for us all to WAKE UP and work together with a BALANCE. I needed to give in and let go of everything I was holding back. I had never thought I could achieve any more of a 'Zen like' state after my experience with ayahuasca in Peru.... until I met ISHTAR.

My book ended. It ended on this chapter and all I knew was that I was Awake and that this chapter was going to take a ton of work to put together... little did I realize it would result in hundreds of hand written pages and drawings done by myself, done by a blue-eyed girl and I, working in shifts, meditating, finding a balance, and talking to the blue, green, gold, and red eye of beauty that I can only associate the name 'ISHTAR' with it. This eye is also within myself, and it is an eye of compassion, and it is with both of my eyes, I was able to find the Balance to complete this truce; to find the Balance, to love everyone with the same compassion that I love ISHTAR with. The love of a family, the love for oneself, the love for God is ISHTAR. For I know now that we are all one, and we are all God.

   The blue-eyed was an 'empath'... well truly these things do not exist. She was a young adult that had embraced and opened her Right side. She did not know this. I did.

   She was a sponge. She soaked up every person's feelings that she came in contact with. She would hug stranger after stranger, and take away their pain, only to collapse alone in her room, crying. I could not let this happen. My left side saw this and needed to teach her the Balance that I was showing everyone else, yet not embracing myself. She taught me my

I LOVE my brother ENKI

Balance. I taught her hers. A Rick needs their Morty. And that is the truth of it all. That is the balance. It is within us all. It is not found in others until we can find the balance in ourselves.

This young woman was born with undiagnosed alopecia areata. Her hair was pigment-less. It was frail. It did not grow. Her hair extensions were her life. She cherished them as she was unable to grow the head of hair that every women desires. After meeting her, and having the Left side of my soul embraced, she had no effect on me like other men, and we were able to get along as good friends. A Morty needs his Rick.

She had been writing in her journal since moving to Western Canada some months prior, but had awoken her Right side 4 years earlier. The book slowly was filled with drawings and writings that became clearer as we became more Balanced.

Just as my music was screaming at myself to allow my Right side to wake up, her journals were telling her to allow her Left side to awaken as well. Neither of us had the guidance to figure this out on our own, but we had each other. We were opposites. We were the same. We are two different people, fighting individually for inner balance, yet our story is the story of all mankind.

After we started to find the Balance, unreal things began happening. We were connected. We could tell what each other was feeling without speaking. We could communicate without talking. We would know when the other was going to call. We knew when the other was experiencing anxiety.

KN LN

On the 10th of March 2018, this lady found her Balance. I was her coach. I was her mentor. I preached the truth without living it. I lived only for myself and all my compassion was faked in order to get ahead in life. It did not matter if I have been sober for years, or a day, it did not matter if I was living a healthy and active life. Without the Balance of the mind, there is no balance of the body.

When she Woke up the night after finishing the 44 questions with ISHTAR. Her hair was longer, thicker. Her hair was BROWN! Her eyes had lightened up several shades. I was not even surprised. I had meditated off a tattoo that had a significant meaning recently. My body was changing as well. I have become a man, and at the end of my 412th moon. We were fully expecting these changes after the Balance was becoming apparent. All health is Mental. The Universe is Mental. The ALL is MIND.

At this point I want to thank you and I also want to apologize. There is a balance here as well. The first 10 chapters of this book have a role to play. It was written under the half of our soul that is self-righteous. ISHTAR had started to write a book as well, or the start of a Pleiadian propaganda piece

I LOVE my brother ENKI

herself. Both of us are not ashamed, as it is a part of all of us. It is a part of us that needs to come out and be expressed. It is different for each of us. It is just part of our story.

There has been a tipping point. There is now a Truce. The tipping point has occurred and it is now a time for unity. It is a time for love. And it is also a time for individuality. Is the drill bit or the on/off switch more important in the machine? Moving forward we do not have to spread hate. We all need the Balance.

If you are reading this as someone who believes they are WOKE, then please move forward with a new light. Move forward seeking the Balance. Identify what is holding you back as an individual and join the community as a member that has a unique grouping of experiences to offer.

If you are reading this as someone who does not understand the meaning of WOKE, then please meditate on the duality, and the oneness that can be found when taking a step back to look within.

I LOVE my brother ENKI

KN LN

I LOVE my brother ENKI

We wrote this for us.
We are one.
N

KN LN

I LOVE my brother ENKI

"*The Crossed Keys*", 'A follow up, for times have changed', by
KN LN, coming soon.

The current state of our existence has changed. The
last 100 years has produced little in the way of Evidence of True
change to the psyche of MAN. It was not until recently that a
significant change has undergone to Humanity as a whole. The
existing books that I have commanded to be written are
outdated. Not just in the upkeep with Science and the current
state of KIA, but outdated in the progression of the 5th RACE of
MAN. The beings from the previous Races, that exist at higher
frequencies, higher Planes of Existence, are deeply tied to the
progression of this 5th Grand Cycle. A cycle that is about to
end. An ending where the general populous has been kept
vastly in the dark for the last 500 years, they have now begun
to AWAKE. MAN has begun to remember...

KN LN

I LOVE my brother ENKI

KN LN